Baby Hugs

by **Dave Ross**

Creator of

A Book of Hugs *and* More Hugs!

Thomas Y. Crowell   New York

For Baby Tara

Baby Hugs
Copyright © 1987 by David H. Ross
All rights reserved. No part of this book may be
used or reproduced in any manner whatsoever without
written permission except in the case of brief quotations
embodied in critical articles and reviews. Printed in
the United States of America. For information address
Thomas Y. Crowell Junior Books, 10 East 53rd Street,
New York, N.Y. 10022. Published simultaneously in
Canada by Fitzhenry & Whiteside Limited, Toronto.
10 9 8 7 6 5 4 3 2 1
First Edition

Library of Congress Cataloging-in-Publication Data
Ross, Dave, 1949–
  Baby hugs.

  Summary: Describes different ways to hug a baby,
including gotcha hugs, storytime hugs, and family hugs.
  [1. Hugging—Fiction. 2. Babies—Fiction]
I. Title.
PZ7.R71964Bad 1987   [E]   87-498
ISBN 0-694-00221-6
ISBN 0-690-04639-1 (lib. bdg.)

You can hug a lot of things…

but everyone agrees the best hugs of all are when you hug a baby.

Babies are soft and warm, smell good (most of the time), and soon learn to hug you back.

Baby hugs are very important...

Along with food and shelter, love and hugs are essential to the health and happiness of a baby.

In baby language, a hug means "I LOVE YOU!" And that's something you can tell a baby over...

and over   and over   and over.

Baby hugs are good for everyone.

In fact, it is almost impossible to frown while hugging a baby.

Newborn Hugs

This is baby's very first hug.

Everyone works hard for Newborn Hugs.

There are hugs to welcome the new adopted baby, too.

Meet-the-New-Baby Hugs

Grandparent Hugs

Big Brother/
Big Sister Hugs

Uncle Jim Hugs

Aunt Eleanor Hugs

Everybody likes to hug the new baby.

Neighbors

The Mail Carrier

Office Buddies

Feeding Hugs

Nursing Hugs

These are special hugs just for Mommy and baby.

The 3 A.M. Feeding Hug

The Cereal & Mixed Vegetable Hug

Burp-the-Baby Hugs

There are two basic Burp-the-Baby Hugs.

Over-the-Shoulder Burp-the-Baby Hug

Over-the-Arm Burp-the-Baby Hug

CAUTION
Some Burp-the-Baby Hugs
produce surprising results.
Proper attire is suggested.

Two other kinds of hugs that may be hazardous to your wardrobe:

Teething Hug

Leaky-Diaper Hug

(Some kinds of hugs can't be postponed!)

Wake-Up Hugs

(Also known as Good-Morning Hugs)

Most Wake-Up Hugs happen between the crib and the changing table.

Extended Good-Morning Hugs are useful for when baby wakes up at 5 A.M. on Sunday.

Hugs for Going Places

Shoulder-Ride Hug

Carrier Hugs

Bicycle Hug

Juggle Hugs

Checkout Hugs

Laundromat Hugs

Juggle Hugs can also be useful at home.

The Daddy's-Little-Helper Hug

The Telephone-and-Door-Stretch Hang-On Hug

Play Hugs

Flying Hug

Toe Hugs

This little piggy went to market.
This little piggy stayed home.
This little piggy had roast beef.
This little piggy had none…

and this little piggy went
wee
wee
wee
all the way home.

Knee-Ride Hug

Come-and-Get-Me Hug

Gotcha Hug

Baby-Sitter Hugs

Comfort Hugs

Cranky Baby Hugs

There are two basic Comfort Hugs for a cranky baby.
(Both involve a lot of back-patting.)

The Walking Hug

The Rocking Hug

Things to say while
hugging a cranky baby:

"Awwwww"
"Whatsamatter, Baby?"
"Neee Neee Naaa Naaa"
(Repeat as needed.)

Sick Baby Hugs

Boo-boo Hugs

...the best medicine for
minor injuries.
(May be administered
with a kiss.)

Panic Hugs

Sometimes Panic Huggers have to be peeled off.

Family Hugs

The Add-On Hug

The Sandwich Hug

The Reach-Around Hug

Whole-Family Hugs

These pass-the-baby hugs are especially common
on holidays or at family reunions.

Multiple-Baby Hugs

Double your pleasure
with a **Twin Hug**.

A **Three-Baby Hug**
is a Triple Play.

For quintuplets
or more,
assistants may be
required.

Hugs to End the Day With

Bath-Time Hugs

Soapy Baby Hug
Sometimes baby needs
a hug before
the bath is over.

Towel Hug
These dry-off hugs are for baby *and* bath-giver.

Story-Time Hugs

Story-Time Hugs are best just before bedtime.

Good-Night Hugs

There is no such thing as one Good-Night Hug.

Hug Strategies

Babies have many ways of asking for hugs.

Physical

Yoo-hoo Tug   **Leg Grab**   **Climb-Up Cuddle**

Psychological

Flirting   **Lip Quivering**   **Crying**

Baby Hug Facts & Hints

A baby that gets lots of hugs will give lots of hugs.

Besides their mommies, daddies, grandparents, etc., babies love to hug...
teddy bears of all sizes
gentle pets
other babies
& blankies.

(Keep them away from skunks, freshly painted lawn furniture, and rosebushes.)

Hugging a baby is an investment that guarantees a lifetime of hugs in return.

Rules for Hugging Babies

1. Hug happy babies.

2. Hug cranky babies.

3. Hug sick babies.

4. When in doubt, hug the baby!

5. Always remember,
a baby *never* outgrows
the need for hugs.